This book was written in collaboration with,
and in loving memory of, my mother Ruth Reid.

www.mascotbooks.com

The High-Flying Adventures of Luke and Dancing Duke

For more information, please contact:
Mascot Books
620 Herndon Parkway, Suite 320
Herndon, VA 20170
info@mascotbooks.com

Library of Congress Control Number: 2020906360

CPSIA Code: PRT0121A
ISBN-13: 978-1-64543-188-6

Printed in the United States

The HIGH-FLYING ADVENTURES of LUKE and DANCING DUKE

ROBERT REID AND RUTH REID
ILLUSTRATED BY WALTER POLICELLI

"Today, class," Ms. Krinkle said, "we'll learn about when barnstormers filled the sky. These aerial daredevils performed astounding tricks way up high."

"Duke, imagine if we were famous barnstormers! How cool would that be?" Luke drifts off to sleep with Duke by his side and begins to dream...

Buzz, buzz, buzz! Whirr, whirr, whirr!

Soaring high above the clouds, the Red Baron flew.
Its engines made a familiar sound, one the town all knew.

It meant Luke and Duke were fast on their way
to thrill the crowd that autumn day.

Barnstormers they're called, courageous and brave.
They'd fly through a barn door with a smile and wave.

Spins and swoops, loop-the-loops, and wing-walking too.
Daring dives and barrel rolls, to name just a few.

Flying way up into the brilliant blue sky,
they soared over rolling green pastures and folks waving hi.

With Luke keeping it steady,
Duke walked out on the wing real slow.
Then he balanced on his front paws,
to give the crowd a real show.

In the evening as the sun sank low,
Luke and Duke prepared for their show.

Washing off mud, bugs, and grime,
the plane dazzled, with a sparkling shine.

Then, just moments before the show,
dark clouds formed and a strong wind began to blow.

As the plane rose skyward, the wings began to shake.
"Don't worry," Luke said. "We've been through worse,
for goodness' sake."

The plane zigzagged and looped and circled above,
while Luke waved to the crowd, his hand in a glove.

It was time for Duke to step out on the wing,
when a great gust of wind gave a whistling ring.

They struggled to stay up, but the wind was too strong.
A hush descended on the crowd. Something was terribly wrong!

With parachutes secure, and on the count of three,
Luke and Duke jumped from the Red Baron for all to see.

They opened their parachutes and floated gently to the ground.
When Luke landed, he looked all around.

"Duke! Duke!" he cried out loud.
But all he heard was a sigh from the crowd.

"Please, please, can you help me find Duke?"
"Of course we will," the townsfolk comforted Luke.

Through fields they searched, and pastures they combed,
but finding no sign of Duke, they sadly went home.

That night, Luke was very sad.
Tossing and turning, a sleepless night he had.

He dreamed of Duke—
all alone, hurt, or in harm.
Then he jolted up with a thought:
We didn't search the Wicks's farm!

Luke quickly got dressed and raced across town.
Outside the farmhouse, Farmer Wicks was sitting down.

"Mr. Wicks, Mr. Wicks, have you seen my dog, Duke?"
"No," he said, "but feel free to look around, Luke."

He walked through the apple orchard, its branches so bare,
hoping to see Duke and his tangled parachute there.

To the cornfields and the hilly pumpkin patch he climbed.
With morning fast approaching,
Luke knew he was running out of time.

Then from the barn—a soft barking he heard!
His steps quickened as he followed it as fast as he could.

Inside the barn, he looked frantically through stacks of hay,
and that's when he found Duke, his fur a mess, but otherwise okay.

The news spread quickly—Duke had been found!
A crowd gathered to cheer when they arrived back in town.

Luke thanked everyone and announced for all to hear,
"The high-flying duo will be back!" he promised. "Next year!"

"Luke, school time!" His mom shook him awake. "It's time to go."

"I can't," he mumbled. "We have to get ready for the show."

"A show?" his mom asked. "You're confused, I think."

"Oh, uh, maybe I am," Luke said with a wink.

Ruth Reid was a devoted mother and wife who always had a desire to write. One day while reading the newspaper, she read an article that quickly captured her attention and imagination. This was the spark that led her to writing her very first children's book. She quickly realized that while this story would be very entertaining, it would also be educational, teaching children about a special time in our nation's history when barnstormers filled the sky, performing their aerial stunts.

Robert Reid shared his mother's passion for creative pursuits and recognized the appeal of her story to children. His was a labor of love, and he worked on the original manuscript to bring his mother's vision to reality. She passed away in 2017 and he knows she would have been very proud to see the book completed.